Walt Disney's
DUMBO

Adapted by Teddy Slater
Illustrated by Ron Dias and
Annie Guenther

A GOLDEN BOOK · NEW YORK

Western Publishing Company, Inc., Racine, Wisconsin 53404

Dumbo, Mrs. Jumbo's baby boy, was the littlest elephant in the whole circus. He had a cute little trunk, a short little tail, and two of the biggest, floppiest ears ever.

Mrs. Jumbo thought everything about her son was just perfect. But everyone else thought his ears were just plain ridiculous. The audience sneered at him, and the other elephants scorned him.

Those big ears kept getting poor Dumbo into big trouble. The first time Dumbo lined up in the circus parade with the other elephants, he tripped over his own ears. The other elephants did not think that was very funny!

Later, a bunch of bullies came to the circus. First they teased Dumbo. When they got tired of that, they began to pinch and poke him. When one of the boys pulled his tail—hard!—Dumbo couldn't help but yell.

Dumbo's mother ran to the rescue and gave that
bully the spanking he deserved.

The bully cried, "Help! Help! Wild elephant!" The
audience panicked and raced for the exits. Circus
guards surrounded Mrs. Jumbo and tied her up.

"Put that beast in the prison car before she
tramples all our customers," the ringmaster ordered.

So the guards threw poor Mrs. Jumbo into a
locked cage.

Without his mother to protect him, Dumbo's life was harder than ever. The other elephants blamed Dumbo's big ears for giving them and Mrs. Jumbo a bad name.

Luckily Timothy Q. Mouse believed that the other elephants were wrong about Dumbo. Timothy decided to be Dumbo's friend. He would try to help Dumbo prove he was a good elephant.

One day the ringmaster decided to put Dumbo in a brand-new act, the Great Pyramid. After the other elephants had formed a big pyramid, Dumbo would leap off a springboard and land on its very top.

Dumbo practiced long and hard. But no matter what he did, his floppy ears kept falling over his eyes. Timothy took care of that. "We'll just tie your ears in a knot," he said. "That should keep them out of your way."

All went well until the first show. Dumbo's heart
was pounding as he ran into the center ring. Suddenly
Dumbo's ears came undone, and he tripped over
them, flying right into the teetering pyramid of
elephants. Crash! Smash! All the elephants came
tumbling down.

The ringmaster was so angry that he threatened to
send Dumbo to a zoo. But when he calmed down a
bit, he decided instead to make Dumbo a clown. After
all, the ringmaster thought, the funny-looking
elephant would surely be able to make people laugh.

The clowns made Dumbo the butt of all their jokes. They set off firecrackers under his feet and threw pies in his face. They tripped him and teased him. To top it off, they decided to dress Dumbo like a baby and make him jump out of a fake burning building.

Dumbo soon found himself trembling on top of the fake building, while fake fire fighters clowned below. Too scared to jump, Dumbo felt the hot flames at his feet. Then he felt a shove from behind as one of the clowns pushed him out of the open window. Down, down Dumbo fell—through the fire fighter's safety net and into a tub of mud.

The audience laughed and laughed, but Dumbo felt
like crying. To cheer him up, Timothy suggested that
they visit Mrs. Jumbo. Late that night the two pals
sneaked over to the prison car. Mrs. Jumbo stuck
her trunk out through the bars and gave her boy a
big hug.

"Don't let the hard times get you down," she told
Dumbo. "Just do your best, and someday you'll be
flying high."

By the time Dumbo left his mother, he was feeling
much better. With Timothy tucked snugly into his
cap, Dumbo strolled into the countryside. Far into the
night Dumbo frolicked in the moonlight.

The next thing Timothy knew, it was morning. He was surprised to find that he and Dumbo weren't in their circus tent, or even on the ground. They were perched on a high branch of a very tall tree. And they weren't alone. On a nearby branch sat a whole flock of crows.

When Dumbo woke up, he was surprised, too. He fell right out of the tree and into a shallow pond.

"I wonder how we ever got up there," Timothy said.

"There's only one way up," the biggest crow said. "You must have flown."

"But we don't know how to fly," Timothy protested.

"It's easy," the crow replied. "Just flap your wings." The bird pointed to Dumbo's big ears.

Timothy thought flying could be Dumbo's chance to prove he was a star elephant. But Dumbo didn't remember flying, and he didn't think he could do it again.

"If you need a little help," a crow said, "take this." He handed Dumbo a shiny black feather. "It's magic," the crow explained. "Hold on to this and you can't help but fly."

Dumbo took the magic feather in his trunk and began to flap his ears while the whole crew of crows circled around him, offering advice.

Faster and faster Dumbo flapped, but his feet
remained planted firmly on the ground.

"Come on, Dumbo," Timothy urged. "You just
need to get a good start." Timothy and the crows led
Dumbo up to a high ledge. The little elephant again
began flapping his ears, and the crows gave him a
gentle push.

Suddenly Dumbo was in the air. At first he was
scared, and he almost crashed. But then he
remembered his magic feather. He spread his big ears
and suddenly he was flying like a bird. He swooped
and he soared. What fun it was to fly!

After thanking the crows, Dumbo and Timothy
headed back to the circus. They got there just as
Dumbo's act was about to begin. Once more Dumbo
found himself atop a burning building. Once more he
was pushed through the window. But this time it was
Dumbo who had the last laugh, for instead of
dropping like a stone into the net, he glided gracefully
up into the air.

As the crowd gasped in amazement Dumbo flew higher and higher. Upside down, right side up—the happy little elephant flew every which way.

Dumbo was having a lot of fun. But suddenly the magic feather slipped from his trunk and fluttered to the ground. Dumbo panicked and began to plummet after it.

Dumbo would have crashed if he hadn't heard
Timothy cry, "Come on, Dumbo. You don't need that
feather to fly. All you need is your own two ears."

Dumbo knew his friend was right. Spreading his big
ears, he hovered just inches from the ground. Then
he gave a mighty flap, and soon he was flying higher
than ever.

From that day on, Dumbo was a star. The ringmaster changed the name of the show to Dumbo's Flying Circus. Dumbo got all the peanuts he could eat, plus a private car on the circus train, where he could be with his mother.

Now all the other elephants tried to stretch their ears so they could be just like Dumbo. It was no use, for there never was and never would be but one flying elephant—Dumbo!